Frederica's New Home

Linda J. Hawkins

Written by Linda J. Hawkins

THE STORY BEHIND THE BOOK

In the 90's my husband and I decided we needed a waterfall and pond added to our flower garden. We enjoyed the new endeavor.

Then someone gave us goldfish that had outgrown their fish tank. My maiden name was Gill, my mother-in-law's name was Goldie, thus the two fish names. Then we had a frog to move in. That frog loved the pond, swimming, the waterfall, the fish, and especially the bugs.

Adventures happened in the months and years that followed, along with daily visits from butterflies, dragonflies and other critters.

Thanks to Carolyn Williams, yes, it finally happened!

Designed by Tonya L Matthews

Dedicated to

Emory Jane

and
all
children.

Every child is important in God's eyes,
no mistakes, no rejecting them.

He would take them up in His arms ... Matthew 18:5
Jesus said, "And whoso shall receive one such
little child in my name received me."

JESUS, loves the little children,
and so does this author.

Dear friend of children,

Learning and loving to read is a great accomplishment for early childhood. We can present our children with interesting materials to make time fun and rewarding.

The following suggestions can enhance this process:

Before reading the book, ask the child to read the title and look at the cover to predict what the story is about.

Read with expression, enjoying this time with your child. Pretend to become the character and express and read the same way the character would express him/herself.

Read a page and allow the child to repeat, mimicking your expressions and inflection.

> "Children are a gift from the Lord; they are a reward from Him."
>
> Psalm 127:3

During the reading, encourage younger children to pick out letters and older children to sound out new words they do not recognize right away.

Help the child to use phonetic skills to sound out new words. Do not pressure the child if they struggle with new words. Offer assistance. They may remember the next time they see it. You want reading time to be a positive experience.

Encourage the child to read to others, brothers, sisters, or to pretend their baby dolls or bears are their audience. They feel grown up while doing this. They can learn while assuming the role of the teacher.

Ask questions about the book, encourage discussion, and laugh together as you share the funny parts of the story. Ask "Did you learn anything new from the book? Who or what was your favorite part? What good or bad decisions were made?"

One hot July day,
Frederica sat staring
across at her home.
The pond was all dried up;
the grass was crunchy
and brown.

Clouds floated overhead,
but they were not rain clouds.
They were big, billowy white clouds.

Frederica sat among pond grasses that rattled from the blowing, hot breeze. "I must find a new home. I cannot stay here another day."

Frederica's friend, Dipper, a dragonfly who was called Dip by his friends, flew around the pond.

He dipped in and out of the many cattails.

Dip asked,
"Why are you
looking sad
today?"

"There is no water left for me to swim. I must find a new home. I do not know where to look," cried Frederica.

Drifting to the cattails, Dip cheerfully said,
"The house on the hill has a lovely goldfish
pond, and it is surrounded by flowers,
and a sparkling waterfall."

Frederica leaped into the air, then sat down. She batted her large round eyes. "Do you suppose I would be welcome there?"

"That is something you must check for yourself," Dip said as he disappeared through the field.

Frederica looked around thinking, "Well, I suppose changes come. I must be on my way. Today is moving day!"

But she suddenly felt sad, again, as she sat looking about her. "I wonder if the house on the hill will let a frog move in?"

She sighed. "Right here is where I was born and lived all my life."

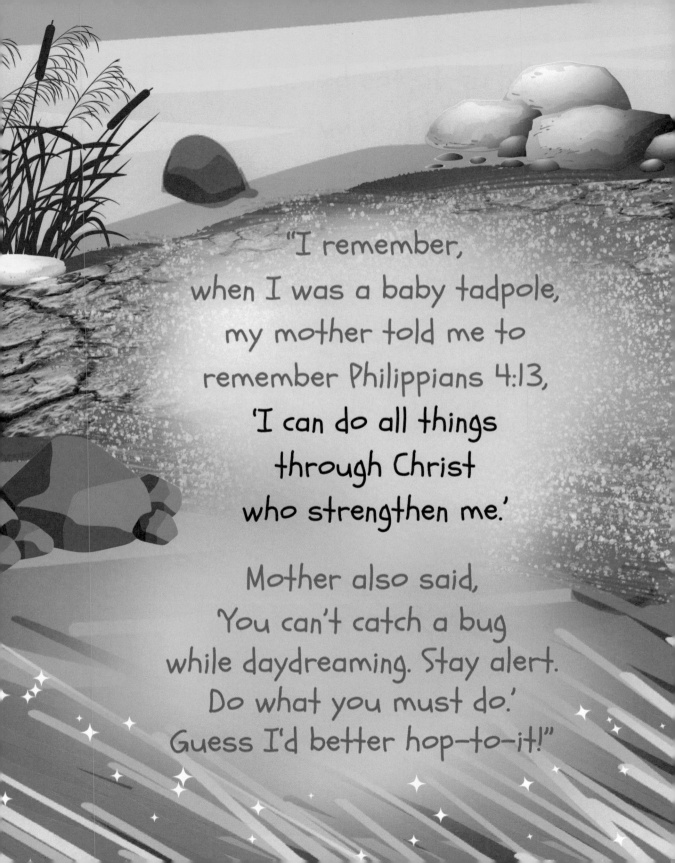

"I remember,
when I was a baby tadpole,
my mother told me to
remember Philippians 4:13,
'I can do all things
through Christ
who strengthen me.'

Mother also said,
You can't catch a bug
while daydreaming. Stay alert.
Do what you must do.'
Guess I'd better hop-to-it!"

The road up to the house was rocky and hot, but Frederica hopped on.

"I need to keep hopping. I have to go check out that pond for myself."

Frederica knew that Dip
had always been her
faithful friend.

Plus, Dip has large eyes.
If he said there is a nice pond,
she believed him. She would find it.

When Frederica arrived, she could not believe her eyes.

"Wow! This is unbelievable. INCREDIBLE! It is even lovelier than dragonfly described."

She saw, Flutter, her butterfly friend, who was rightfully named because she loved to flutter and dance, sipping from one beautiful flower to another.

Frederica gave a big leap and landed on a lily pad. "Oh! How refreshing!"

Water, water, water!

She spoke to Flutter,

"I think this is going to be a wonderful place to live!"

As Frederica climbed up onto the lily pad she heard someone whisper, "There is a noisy frog that jumped right into my path as I swam near the waterfall."

Frederica looked
down to see
two goldfish
swimming
and talking.

"Do not worry Goldie. There is plenty of room for her too," Gills said.

"But, Gills, you do not understand.
That frog might eat all our food.
Then we will not have any,"
replied Goldie.

"You worry too much. Frogs eat bugs but not all of them. Remember, we are to be kind to one another."

Ephesians 4:32

"Yes! Like I said there is room for a frog in this pond."

"I'll show them a hippity-hoppity froggy trick! They will enjoy this," croaked Frederica.

"I will clear the bugs!"

She hopped out of the water and jumped happily around the edges of the pond.

Bugs flew everywhere.

Many bugs fell into the water.
Goldie and Gills filled their tummies
with lots of yummy bugs.
Frederica thought of
Proverbs 18:24,

"To have friends,
we have to show
ourselves friendly.

Cool, I can do this!"

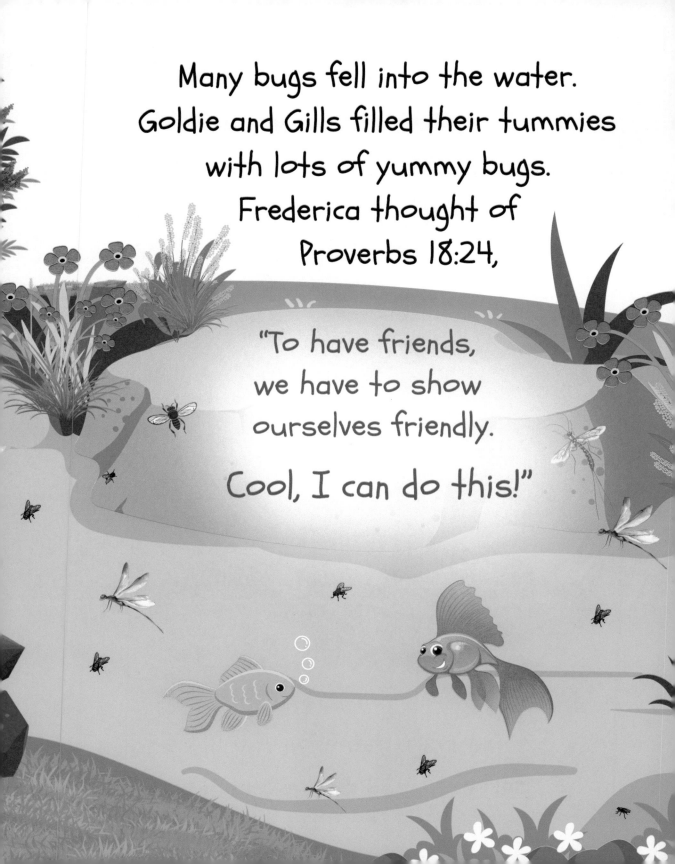

Frederica smiled as the
two fish swam away.

"Sitting right here on my lily pad is the
perfect spot for my evening meal."

"And it will be nice to have goldfish swimming near."

Frederica was happy!

"This is going to be a great place to live."

"I will be the best friend I can be!

I'm so glad Dad taught me the Golden Rule: Do unto others what you'd like to be done unto you." Matthew 7:12

She knew she would not miss the old place because her new home was great, with flowing water, plenty of bugs, and room for all her friends!

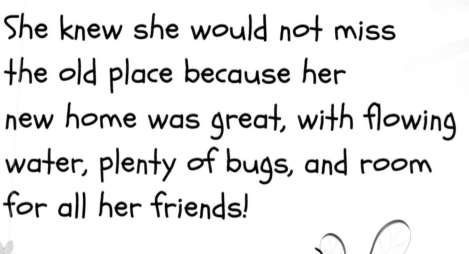

For I know the plans I have for you,
declares the Lord, plans to prosper you
and not to harm you, plans to give
you hope and a future.

Jeremiah 29:11

Ribbit Ribbit

From your Froggy Friend Frederica

ENJOY THIS HANDS—ON PROJECT!

Frog-in-Pond
recipe

This author has prepared this recipe
many times for many children.
May you enjoy this treat for
breakfast/brunch/or snack.

Items needed:
1 slice of bread
1 egg
1 tbs butter
Salt & pepper to taste

Frog-shaped cookie cutter (or use a round one)

Frog cutters are available at various retailer locations
and online. You could pick up one for this recipe, YUMMY!

Children appreciate these added fun times.

**Frogs
are
actually
quite
fascinating.**

**Kids love
learning about
frogs, and
you will too!**

**While you
prepare
this treat,
discuss
fun frog facts
found at**
lindajhawkins.com

1. Cut the center from the bread (frog or circle) and set aside (see #6)

2. Break the egg into a small bowl, add salt/pepper (see options below)

3. Melt butter in skillet, place the outer edge of bread in skillet on the butter

4. Pour beaten egg mixture into the pond (bread), cook on medium heat

5. Cook until mixture is set/bread is brown/flip over, cook the other side

6. Place the center of cut-out bread into toaster/brown/serve with your eggs (Frog-in-Pond)

Options:
Sprinkle shredded cheese, added to the beaten egg mixture. Or, add one drop of green food coloring, or chopped ham, to egg mixture for a fun Green Eggs and Ham meal.

**View food pictures
at lindajhawkins.com**

About the Author

Author Linda J. Hawkins is a lover of nature and all God's wonderful creation. Nature can be our outdoor classroom for teaching our children. Join the author as she not only shares with your child but points them to sage advice from the greatest book ever written: God's Word. It's a time of sharing and caring, as you read with your child. Visit lindajhawkins.com for more children's books, as well as books for all ages such as the award-winning recipe series, *Southern Seasons*.

"God's great big outdoors is surely the most lovely garden and playground of all!"
-- Linda J. Hawkins

ADDITIONAL BOOKS AT LINDAJHAWKINS.COM

Award Winning Author & Photographer

Who Gives a Hoot? Hunter Hoot, the Great Horned Owl

Alexander and the Great Food Fight

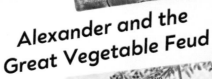

Alexander and the Great Vegetable Feud

Alexander and the Great Berry Patch

Catering to Children: With Recipes for Memorable Tea Parties

AND MANY MORE AT LINDAJHAWKINS.COM

Made in the USA
Columbia, SC
25 April 2024

34734575R00024